the Sun with Loving Light

Waldorf
PUBLICATIONS

Printed with support from the Waldorf Curriculum Fund,
the Waldorf Stiftung, and the Rudolf und Clara Kreutzer-Stiftung

Published by
Waldorf Publications at the
Research Institute for Waldorf Education
351 Fairview Avenue
Hudson, NY 12534

Title: *The Sun with Loving Light*
Editor: Stephen Bloomquist
Illustrations: Pamela Dalton
Music layout: Patrice Maynard
Design & layout: Ann Erwin
Proofreader: Melissa Merkling
Cover illustration: Hawthorne Valley Waldorf School eleventh grade student
Endleaves: Morning and evening watercolors: Schneider, *Sonnenaufgang und Sonnenuntergang*, J. Ch. Mellinger Verlag

ISBN #978-1-936367-63-4

Printed in cooperation with the Bund der Freien Waldorfschulen, based on *Der Sonne Licht*, an original collection by Caroline von Heydebrand for the first Waldorf School, Stuttgart, Germany, and transliterated for North America.

Table of Contents

Beginning / Morning

Autumn

Autumn continued

Winter

Spring

Summer

In Closing

Beginning/Morning

The Sun with Loving Light

The Sun with loving light
Makes bright for me each day.
The soul with spirit power
Gives strength unto my limbs.
In sunlight shining clear
I reverence, O God,
The strength of humankind
Which Thou so graciously
Hast planted in my soul
That I, with all my might,
May love to work and learn.
From Thee stream light and strength.
To Thee rise love and thanks.

– *Rudolf Steiner*
Trans. Arvia MacKaye Ege

America the Beautiful

O beautiful for spacious skies,
For amber waves of grain,
For purple mountain majesties
Above the fruited plain!
America! America!
God shed His grace on thee
And crown thy good with brotherhood
From sea to shining sea!

– *Katharine Lee Bates*

Awake!

Awake! Awake! The day has dawned
On field and stream and golden pond.
The sun has risen o'er the land –
O'er mountain, hill, and seaside strand.
Awake! Awake! It's time to rise
And rub the sleep out of your eyes.
There's much to do and learn today.
So join us in our work and play.

– Stephen Bloomquist

Brave and True

Brave and true I will be.
Each good deed sets me free.
Each kind word makes me strong.
I will fight for the right.
I will conquer the wrong.

God's Gifts

Wherever human beings are,
'Neath Southern Cross or Northern Star,
On mountain top or sandy plain,
God's gifts to us are all the same.

Firm earth beneath our feet He gives,
In heavenly air we breathe and live,
Fire warms us when the wild wind blows,
And for our thirst cool water flows.

Now stone and plant and beast and man
Have lived on Earth since Earth began.
And of all these 'tis Man who gives
His thanks to God for all that lives.

- Dorothy Harrer

Mother Earth

Elisabeth Lebret

How the Earth Came to Be

an Onondaga Tale

Long ago, there was no Earth, only water. It stretched as far as you could see. There were birds and animals swimming in and on top of the water. There were no people there. The only people at that time lived high above in the Sky World. In the middle of the Sky World was a great and lovely tree. It had four great roots that stretched to the north, south, east, and west. From its branches grew all kinds of fruits and flowers.

There was a strong chief in the Sky World whose young wife was expecting a child. One night she dreamed that the great tree was uprooted and that it lay on its side. She told her dream to her husband and he said, "This is a dream of great power. We must do what we can to make it true." The strong chief put his arms around the great tree and lifted with all his might. At last, with one great effort, he pulled up the tree and laid it on its side.

There was now a hole in the Sky World and the young wife came close to look down. She grasped the branches of the tree and leaned far over. She saw the glittering water down below. She saw two white Swans swimming on the water. Then she lost her balance and began to fall. As she fell, she grasped at the great tree's branches but she managed to grab hold of only a handful of seeds. She fell down, down, down. With a great splash she landed in the water.

The two white Swans swam over to her and lifted her up on their wings. "What a strange creature," said the first Swan. "She has no wings and her feet are not webbed. She will not be able to live on the water."

"No," said the second Swan, "but we cannot hold her up much longer. What shall we do?"

Many of the water animals gathered around to give their advice. Finally the Duck spoke. "There is Earth on the bottom, under the water," he said. "I will dive down and bring up some for her." So the Duck dove down deep, but he soon ran out of breath and had to return to the surface.

"Let me try," said the Loon. "I am a great diver." But the Loon too was forced to come back to the surface without reaching the bottom.

Finally, the Muskrat spoke. "I will dive down to get some Earth," she said. She dove down into the darkness. It felt as if her lungs would burst, but she kept going until she felt the Earth at the bottom of the water. She returned to the surface, gasping for breath, with a pawful of Earth.

"She has the Earth!" the animals cried. "But where can we put it?"

"Place it on my back," said a deep voice. They saw that it was Turtle. So the Muskrat climbed onto Turtle's back. She scratched his shell with her claws as she climbed, and the marks are still on his shell today. The bit of Earth fell onto Turtle's back. Right away the bit of Earth began to grow. It grew and it grew until it became the land that we know now.

The two Swans placed the Sky Woman on the Earth. She walked on the Earth and opened her hand, letting the seeds fall. Trees and plants began to grow from those seeds. Life on Earth had begun. And as far as we know, the Earth is still resting on the great Turtle's back.

Gnomes

Crack, crack,
The rock we hack.
Quake, quake,
The mountains shake.
Bang, bang,
Our hammers clang.
In caverns old
We seek the gold.

Action Poem

The little gnomes
Are sitting on their crystal thrones,
The red, blue, yellow precious stones
Are all their homes.

We hammer and polish the gold crystal eyes
That sun, golden sun, can look in from the skies.

We hammer and polish the silvery eyes
That moon, silver moon, can look in from the skies.

We hammer and polish the diamond eyes
That stars, sparkling stars, can look in from the skies.

So all their homes
Are red, blue, yellow precious stones.
They're sitting on their crystal thrones,
The little gnomes.

– Margret Meyerkort

Four Elements

Warmth

The sun shines bright with love for all,
On plant and beast both great and small.
It wakes to life the darkened earth
And warms the little seeds at birth.
The moon and stars make bright the night
And keep us safe till morning light.

Water

Murmuring water rising in fountains,
Tumbling down mountains out to the sea;
Home of the fishes swimming like wishes,
Nourishing water, flowing and free.

Air

Through the trees and the brush
Comes the wind with a rush,
Swirling leaves with a flair,
Lifting birds in the air,
Slowing down to a hush.

Shaking fruit from the trees,
Raising waves on the seas,
Spreading seeds over land,
Bringing clouds to command –
O the wind blows a storm
And is yet just a breeze.

- Karen Weiland

Earth

Now the farmer plows the earth,
Scatters seeds that bring new birth,
Hoes the weeds and prays for rain
And warming sun to swell the grain.
Reapers cut the golden sheaves
When they see the autumn leaves.

- Stephen Bloomquist

Indian Harvest

Ethel Crowninshield | *Traditional American*

Master Hammerling

I am the master Hammerling.
None faster can a hammer swing.
My blows ring out the livelong day,
A lively din they make – and gay!

My name is Nimblefinger.
Among the roots I linger.
Who brings the seeds to light?
It is I, the merry sprite!

And I am a dwarf called Pickelflipp.
With tripping step, I hop and skip.
From out my tiny house I peek
And laugh at people till I shriek!

I sit here quite alone
On my seat of mossy stone,
In my peaky, pointy hat
And think of this and that.

Oh, rat-a-tat,
I rap and tap
But when you look for me,
I'm gone – like that.

O we are dwarfs so tiny.
We've bells all bright and shiny.
But no one hears us,
No one sees us,
(None at all)!
Unless it please us!

– *B. D. Betteridge, after Düstel*

Children's Prayer

Elisabeth Lebret *Elisabeth Lebret*

The Sheepdog

One evening an old sheepdog, the faithful guardian of his master's sheep, was on his way home. Little lapdogs yapped at him in the street.

He trotted on without looking 'round. When he came to the meat stall, the butcher's dog asked him how he could bear such continual barking and why he did not take one of them by the scruff of his neck.

"No," answered the sheepdog. "They do not worry or bite me. I must keep my teeth for wolves."

– *Rudolf Steiner*

The Seasons

Where did old King Winter go
With his robes of swirling snow,
His frosty crown and his icy spear,
And the North Wind whistling in his ear?
He has fled to his blue ice-palace far
On top of the world near the cold North Star.

Who has come to take his place?
Sweet Spring is here with her smiling face,
The warm West Wind blowing in her hair,
Bluebirds and robins around her there.
In her flowing gown of palest green,
She calls all the flowers to meet their Queen.

Who is the Queen so fair and bright,
Wearing a mantle of shining light,
Who follows the footsteps of smiling Spring
And sheds her warm light over everything?
Roses and lilies will bloom for her,
For she is the bright Queen of Summer.

Who chases the Queen of Summer away?
The fiery Dragon of Fall, they say.
He burns all the leaves to red, orange and brown,
And with flaming breath he blows them down,
Leaving the trees all cold and bare
Till the snow of Winter fills the air.

– Dorothy Harrer

Autumn

The Leaf and the Bird

Said a green little leaf to a bird flitting by,
"Kindly tell me, how is it you manage to fly?"
Said the bird to the leaf as she lit on a bough,
"You need only let go and you'll understand how!"

But the leaf was afraid, till one bright autumn day
He forgot to hold on and he sailed far away;
Far away, but alas! He could never return,
For the way to get back he'd neglected to learn.

– Margaret Peckham

Leaves

Adapted from Molly de Havas *Anonymous*

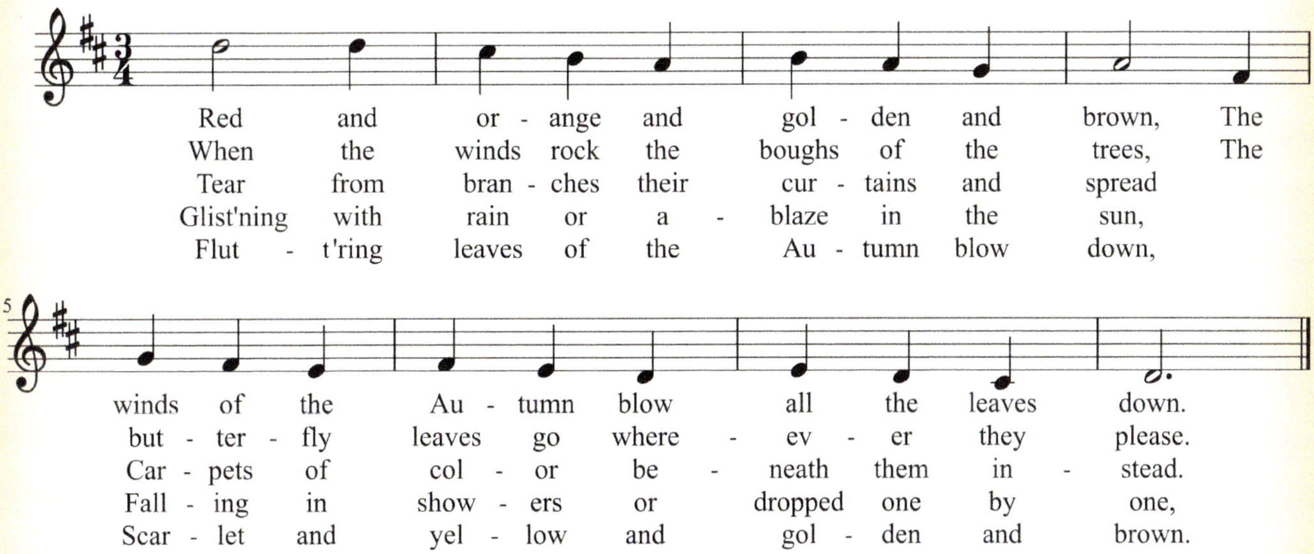

Whisky Frisky

Whisky, frisky,
Hipperty hop,
Up he goes
To the tree top!

Whirly, twirly,
Round and round,
Down he scampers
To the ground.

Furly, curly,
What a tail,
Tall as a feather,
Broad as a sail.

Where's his supper?
In the shell.
Snappy, cracky,
Out it fell.

– *Anonymous*

The Eagle

A man asked the eagle, "Why do you rear your young ones so high up in the air?"

The eagle answered, "If I reared them down on the earth, how would they venture so near to the sun when they are older?"

Land of the Silver Birch

Traditional

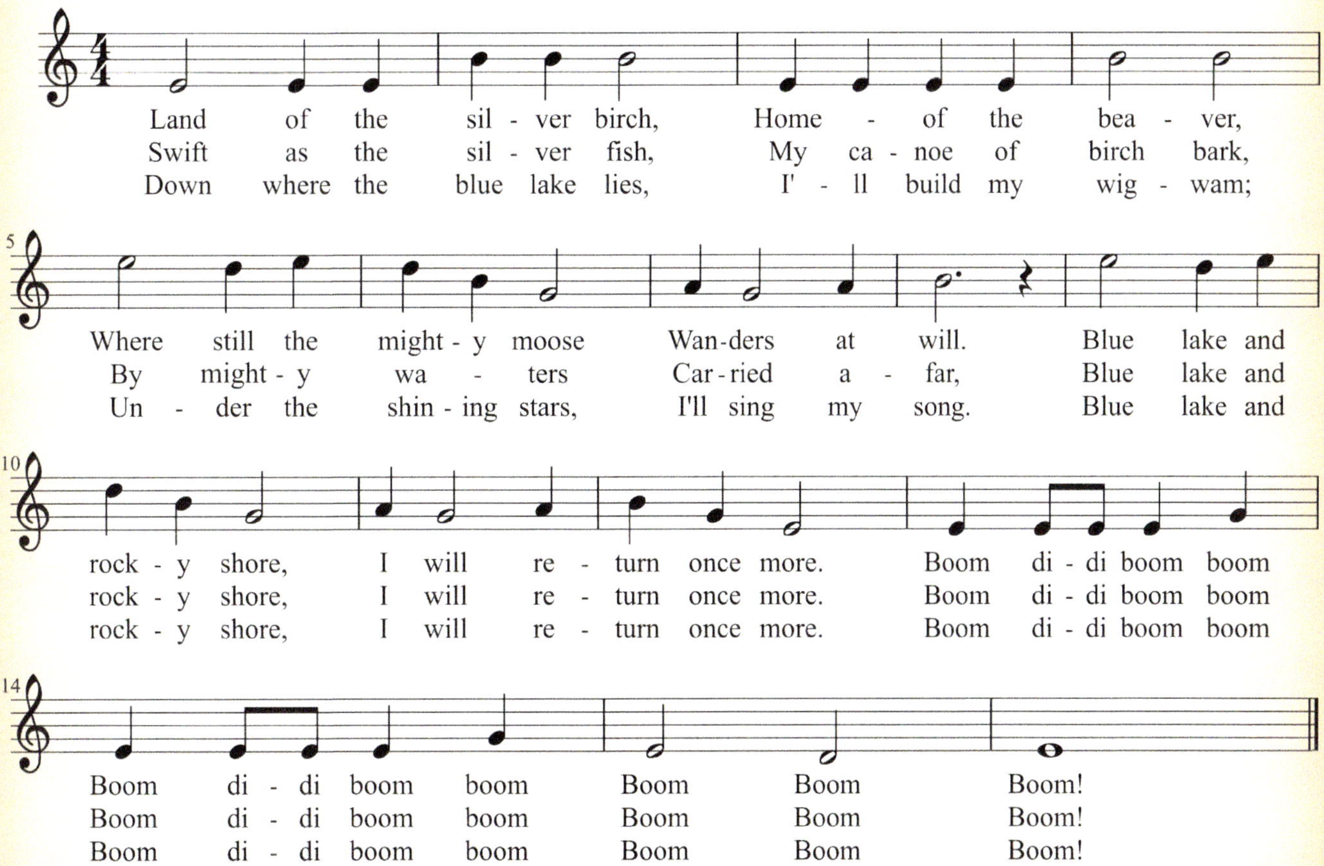

Michaelmas

Elisabeth Lebret *Elisabeth Lebret*

Something Told the Wild Geese

Something told the wild geese it was time to go;
Though the fields were golden, something whispered, "Snow!"

Leaves were green and stirring, berries luster-glossed,
But beneath warm feathers, something cautioned, "Frost!"

All the sagging orchards steamed with amber spice,
But each wild breast stiffened at remembered ice.

Something told the wild geese it was time to fly;
Summer sun was on their wings, Winter in their cry!

- Rachel Field

Cows

Now the gentle cows are standing
Knee-deep in the dewy grass.
Dawn has found them, patient shadows
Watching hours that softly pass.
Moving slowly over meadows,
Munching quiet unhurried ways,
They have naught to do but wander
Down the rich, unheeded days.
Yet they bring about a wonder
Such as not the wisest can,
Changing common meadow grasses
Into richest food of man.
As they lie unmindful, chewing,
By a faintly sounding stream,
What new marvels are they viewing?
What deep secrets do they dream?

- P. S. Moffat

October

Scarlet and yellow and golden and brown,
Winds of October blow all the leaves down;
Tear from the branches their curtains and spread
Carpets of color beneath them instead.
Glistening with rain or ablaze in the sun,
Falling in showers or dropped one by one,
Fluttering leaves of October blow down,
Scarlet and yellow and golden and brown.

– Molly de Havas

Fall

Elisabeth Lebret *Elisabeth Lebret*

The Little Fir Tree and the Pumpkin

There was once a little fir tree who was growing by the side of his mother fir. Every day the little fir looked up to his mother and said, "One day, Mother, I shall be as tall as you are!"

His mother always smiled at him and said, "You grow bigger a little each day."

Behind the fir trees was a great forest. Before them was a farmer's field where many vegetables were growing. In the field grew a patch of pumpkins. The little fir tree looked on in wonder as the pumpkins grew bigger and rounder each day.

One pumpkin heard the fir tree speak to his mother and that pumpkin sneered, "You will never be big. Look at how slowly you grow! While I grow larger and rounder and more golden every day! Ho, ho! You will never grow as fast as I can."

This made the little fir tree feel very sad. Even his mother's smile could not help him to feel better. Every day the pumpkin would laugh at the little fir and show off how much bigger and rounder he had become in a day. Truly, the fir tree could see how fast the pumpkin grew. "Why can't I grow as fast as the pumpkin?" the little fir tree asked his mother.

The mother smiled down on her little tree and said, "Don't listen to the pumpkin, my child. To be strong is to grow slowly. Watch each day and see."

So the little fir tree watched each day. He could see how fast the pumpkin grew. The laughter and boasting of the big, round pumpkin never stopped, and the little fir tree tried very hard not to listen. Some days though, this was hard, and he was very sad at his own slow growth.

One day it grew colder. The wind blew through the branches of the fir trees, and the little fir tree laughed as the wind tickled his needles.

The pumpkin started his usual boasting. On this day the farmer came and began picking the vegetables from his field. He took many vegetables from the field but not the big, round, orange pumpkin. The boasting pumpkin told the little fir tree, "Soon the farmer will take me to market where all will admire my big, round self!"

The farmer did not return. Day after day the pumpkin grew rounder and said over and over that he would soon be the star of the market. The little fir felt very bad that he would not be admired at market, as the pumpkin would be. His mother sang a song of the wind, a song of many years and steady strength, and this soothed the little fir tree.

One day the little fir tree saw the sun peek over the hill. He shook his branches to wake up and heard the sound of a lark and saw her rise high in the air in the morning sun. "Ah!" cried the little fir tree, "the birds are singing their morning song." It was then he realized that he could not hear the sound of the pumpkin, boasting and making him feel sad and small. He looked and saw the pumpkin in his usual place. As he looked closely he saw that the pumpkin had grown so big and round that he had burst. A great split in his side had ended him.

The fir tree was shocked! His mother only smiled and sang her soft song about steady, slow growing. She sang of little trees who grow to be huge and quiet and strong. On that day the little fir tree understood her song in a new way!

Five Little Pumpkins

Traditional

Tonight Is Hallowe'en

Tonight is the night when dead leaves fly
Like witches on switches across the sky,
When elf and sprite flit through the night on a moony sheen.

Tonight is the night when leaves make a sound
Like a gnome in his home under the ground,
When spooks and trolls creep out of holes, mossy and green.

Tonight is the night when pumpkins stare
Through sheaves and leaves everywhere,
When ghoul and ghost and goblin host
Dance round their queen. It's Hallowe'en!

– *Harry Behn*

Goblins

Digging down to deepest dark and danger,
Gleeful goblins gather glistening gold.
High and hard a hundred heavy hammers
Clang and clash in columned caverns cold.
Little lamps their lengthy labors lighten,
Shifting shadows show and shimmering shine
While they ceaselessly search for silver secrets –
Midget men beneath the mountain mine.

– *Molly de Havas*

November

November days are calm and chill,
The mists drift gently down;
The grass is spread with silver webs
And new-dug earth glows brown.
The bare black branches wetly gleam,
The woods in stillness stand;
The yellow sun floats pale and cool
Above the sleeping land.
But Springtime comes again each year,
Again the earth will live,
And bees and plants and flowers will wake
And all their sweetness give.

– *Molly de Havas*

November

Elisabeth Gmeyner — *Elisabeth Lebret*

The North Wind and the Sun

The North Wind and the Sun were disputing which was the stronger. Suddenly they saw a traveller coming down the road, and the Sun said: "I see a way to decide our dispute. Whichever of us can cause that traveller to take off his cloak shall be regarded as the stronger. You may go first."

So the Sun retired behind a cloud, and the Wind began to blow as hard as he could upon the traveller and nearly tore the cloak from its fastenings. But the harder the Wind blew, the more tightly did the traveller wrap his cloak 'round him, till at last the Wind had to give up in despair.

Then the Sun came out and shone in all his glory upon the traveller, who soon found it too hot to walk with his cloak on.

Silver Mists Are Swirling

Silver mists are swirling
Over hill and vale.
I see fingers curling
Through the sunlight pale.
Mellow fruits are ripening
Among the dancing leaves.
The last warmth appearing
Red, amber, golden sheaves.
Now the winds are blowing.
Leaves begin to fall.
Floating orange feathers
Cover nature's hall.
Tiny creatures seeking
A place for winter deep,
Called by Mother Earth
Who her winter watch will keep.
Loving arms enfolding
Each tiny seed below,
Deep in winter's slumber
'Neath field and field of snow.

– A. Grout

Squirrel Nutkin

Francis B. Wood | *Spanish Folk Tune*

Saint Francis and the Wolf of Gubbio

Not very far from Assisi was a little town called Gubbio, where Saint Francis sometimes used to stay. Once when he went there, he found the people panic-stricken, for a huge and fierce wolf had taken up his abode in the neighborhood. The wolf was so bold that it came prowling 'round the walls, ready to seize any person who might be walking there. Once or twice it had even come into the town itself and carried off a little child. No man dared venture abroad unless he were armed; women and children remained at home.

Saint Francis felt sorry for the people, and he decided to go to find the wolf, though the citizens begged him not to attempt it. He left the town, entrusting his life to God.

As Francis approached its lair, the wolf fiercely rushed towards him, with open mouth and angry eyes. At the sight a loud cry rose up from the people who stood watching at a distance.

Unafraid, Saint Francis waited till the creature came quite near. Then he made the sign of the cross over him and said, "Come hither, Brother Wolf. I command thee, in the name of God, to do no harm, neither to me nor to anyone."

Then a great awe fell on the watching people, for the fierce beast instantly shut its mouth, the anger died out of its eyes, and like a lamb it came and lay down at Saint Francis' feet. And Saint Francis went on, "Brother Wolf, much damage have you wrought. You do much evil when you kill the creatures of God without His permission.

"Much terror and sorrow have you caused in the little city, for which you deserve to be slain. But I believe that you have done all this because you were hungry and had nothing to eat. So now will I make peace between you and the citizens of Gubbio. They will provide you with food, on condition you will promise to do no harm to either man or beast. Will you promise?"

In answer the wolf bowed his head, then lifted his big paw and put it into Saint Francis' hand, in token that he promised.

Then Saint Francis bade him return with him to Gubbio and there to renew the promise in the sight of all the people. And the wolf, having made signs that he agreed, trotted along quietly by his side, through the vineyards and along the road which led into the city.

As the news spread, all the people of the town – men and women and children – crowded to the marketplace to see Saint Francis and the wolf. When everybody was gathered together, Saint Francis turned to the people and said, "Brother Wolf has promised to make peace with you and do you no more harm. I will pledge my word for him. Will you on your part promise to feed him and be kind to him?"

Everyone promised to do so. Then Francis turned to the wolf, "Brother Wolf, will you now promise to make peace with these people and to attack neither man nor beast?" And once more the wolf bowed his head and placed his great paw in Saint Francis' hand.

After that the wolf lived two more years in Gubbio and used to walk about like a tame creature from door to door, doing hurt to no one and no one doing hurt to him. He was kindly fed by the people, and as he walked about the town, never a dog barked at him.

At last, after two years, Brother Wolf died of old age. The citizens grieved much, for when they beheld him thus tamely going about, they remembered better the virtues and holiness of Saint Francis.

Windy Nights

Whenever the moon and stars are set,
    Whenever the wind is high,
All night long in the dark and wet,
    A man goes riding by.
Late in the night when the fires are out,
    Why does he gallop and gallop about?

Whenever the trees are crying aloud
    And ships are tossed at sea,
By, on the highway, low and loud,
    By at the gallop goes he.
By at the gallop he goes, and then
    By he comes back at the gallop again.

– Robert Louis Stevenson

For the Golden Corn

E. Smith

Gould

Winter

Snowflakes

Snow flakes falling 'round and 'round,
Falling softly without sound,
Fluttering gently to the ground,
Slowly piling mound on mound.

Tiny crystal stars so white
Give a luster to the night,
Shining in the pale moonlight,
Making even darkness bright.

Frozen water by the mill,
Skaters take a slippery spill.
Skiing through the forest still,
Sledders tumble down the hill.

When the wind begins to blow,
Whirling little flakes of snow,
Rosy cheeks and fingers glow.
Winter is the best I know.

– Stephen Bloomquist

The Moon

From "Das Brünnlein singt und saget"
Trans: Lyn Wilwerth

Elisabeth Lebret

The Town Mouse and the Country Mouse

The Town Mouse went to visit the Country Mouse, who fed her on acorns, nuts, seeds, and whatever she could find. The Town Mouse said, "This is poor fare. Come with me. I will find enough dainties for both of us."

The Country Mouse agreed and they set out together for the town. When they arrived, they went straight to the larder of a big house, where they found bread, meat, bacon, sausages, cheese, and whatever else a mouse could wish for. The Town Mouse said, "Now eat and be of good cheer. Such dishes I have every day in plenty."

Suddenly they heard a clattering of keys. The cook was at the door! The mice were frightened and ran away. The Town Mouse soon found her hole, but the Country Mouse did not know where to go. She ran along the wall to and fro and barely escaped with her life.

When the cook had gone, the Town Mouse said, "Now we will enjoy ourselves. There is no more danger."

But the Country Mouse answered, "It is all very well for you to say. You knew where to hide. But I nearly died of fright. You can stay here in a rich town house and eat your sausages and bacon. I will remain a poor Country Mouse and eat my acorns. You are never safe from the cook, the cat, the traps. The whole house is your enemy. I want to be back at home, safe and free in my little hole in the fields."

A Sledding Song

Sing a song of winter,
    Of frosty clouds in air!
Sing a song of snowflakes,
    Falling everywhere.
Sing a song of winter!
    Sing a song of sleds!
Sing a song of tumbling
    Over heels and heads.
Up and down a hillside
    When the moon is bright,
Sledding is a tiptop
    Wintertime delight.

– Norman C. Schlichter

Look at the Snow

Eleanor Winship

The Snowflake

by Dorothy Harrer

(adapted from "Snow" by Marcia Dodwell)

Clear, glistening Little Drop of Water was rushing and playing and racing down the hill with all his brothers to the sea. A great wave rose and caught them all and threw them into the air so fast that they all shouted and laughed with joy. High in the air, Little Drop of Water hung for a moment but didn't have time to fall back into the sea, for three bright Sun Fairies fanned him with their wings, and up - up - up he rose, so far and so high that he was soon in the sky, way above the highest mountain.

It was cold up there, so cold that Little Drop of Water froze. He couldn't run and spill anymore! He tried to go down and up, forward and backward, right and left, and each time he moved in each direction, he froze in that direction until he was like a tiny, six-pointed star.

All around him, his many brothers had likewise become six-pointed stars, just like him and yet *not* like him, for every single one was formed in a different pattern. They all admired each other so much that they couldn't decide which one was the most beautiful. And what's more, they could float in the air like feathers. Here and there — wherever the Wind blew them — they floated.

They let the Wind carry them a long, long way, until they bumped into Big Old Mountain, who refused to get out of the way.

If the Wind wanted to get by him, he would have to blow either around him or over him. Nor did Big Old Mountain even say, "Excuse me." With a shriek and a whistle, the Wind blew up one side and down the other and, in passing, left all the beautiful, six-pointed Snowflakes on the top of Big Old Mountain. The Mountain suddenly looked like an old, old giant with very white hair, for piles and piles of snowflakes covered his head.

There the Snowflakes lay and rested for many days. They knew they did not want to stay there forever. At last they wished they could be on their way. Sure enough, the Sun rose very much earlier one morning and said, "The days are going to be longer now for a while, and my child, the Earth, is going to be warmed and comforted."

As the Sun's light fell on the Snowflakes, they suddenly slipped down from the mountaintop. They began to run and roll and, sure enough, they had turned into drops of water again. All together they poured down the side of Big Old Mountain in a pure, sweet stream of water, laughing and gurgling with joy and gladness. Those who could listen heard the voice of the water singing: "Gloria, Gloria."

Now, what do you suppose Little Drop of Water, who had been a Snowflake, did next? He slipped underground until he was out of sight. There, underneath the Earth, an old, old Gnome picked him up and carried him to a little seedling who was thirsty.

"Drink," said the old Gnome to the Seedling. "This pure, clear Little Drop of Water will help you to grow."

"I will carry him up to the beautiful Sun," answered Little Wheat Sprout.

So Little Drop of Water entered into Little Wheat Sprout and slowly, slowly rose up in her as she grew taller and taller. At last he entered into a tiny grain of the Wheat that formed at the end of her stalk – up in the sunshine, above the ground. He felt very proud and noble because the Wheat had wrapped him around with a beautiful, green jacket, and as the Sun shone down on him, the green turned to a glorious gold, the very color of the Sun itself.

One day the farmers came to harvest the Wheat. All the Wheat in the field was filled with joy now that the time had come for it all to be made into bread, which would bring life and strength to human beings. And in each grain of Wheat, bearing the pureness and goodness of Heaven from which they came, many Little Drops of Water lay waiting to enter into the bread.

So the Wheat was harvested and threshed, and the golden grains were brought to the mill to be ground into flour. And so the flour was mixed and kneaded and baked into a loaf of golden bread.

And even today, little "snowflake water drops" are hiding in the golden loaves that we eat, and this nourishes each little child who comes into the world.

The Tailor

I saw a little tailor sitting stitch-, stitch-, stitching,
Cross-legged on the floor of his kitch-, kitch-, kitchen.
His thumb and his fingers were so nim-, nim-, nimble
With his wax and his scissors and his thim-, thim-, thimble.

His silk and his cotton he was thread-, thread-, threading
For a gown and a coat for a wed-, wed-, wedding.
His needle flew as swift as a swal-, swal-, swallow,
And his spools and his reels had to fol-, fol-, follow.

He hummed as he worked a little dit-, dit-, ditty:
"The bride is as plump as she's pret-, pret- pretty.
I wouldn't have her taller or short-, short-, shorter.
She can laugh like the falling of the wa-, wa-, water.

"She can put a cherry pie toge-, ge-, gether.
She can dance as light as a fea-, fea-, feather.
She can sing as sweet as a fid-, fid-, fiddle,
And she's only twenty inches 'round the mid-, mid-, middle."

The happy little tailor went on stitch-, stitch-, stitching.
The black and the white in his kitch-, kitch-, kitchen.
He will wear the black one, she will wear the white one,
And the knot the parson ties will be a tight, tight, tight one.

- Eleanor Farjeon

Cooperation

A tale told by the Buddha

Long ago, a hunter went out in search of quail. This hunter could whistle so as to imitate the call of the quail so that every quail who heard him would fly toward the sound of his whistle. The hunter went into the forest and whistled. He waited for the quail to flock to him. When they had gathered around him, he threw his net over them and carried them home with him. He fed them until they were fat and then he sold them at market.

This went on for quite a while until one day, old Grandfather Quail called the quail all together. "Listen," he said, "this hunter is killing us off by the dozens. We must do something to stop him."

"But what can we do?" asked the other quail. "His whistle is so clever that none of us can tell it from a true quail call."

"I have a plan," said Grandfather Quail. "When he throws the net over you, each one of you must poke your head through a hole in the net. Then, on the count of three, all of you must flap your wings in unison, rise up, and fly to the nearest thorn bush. Let the net fall over the thorns and slip your heads out of the holes. The net will stay stuck and you will land on the ground. Then fly away and escape!"

"Yes, yes!" all the quail agreed.

The very next day the hunter returned to the woods. He whistled his quail call and many quail flocked to him – only to have the net thrown over them. But this time the quail knew what to do. Each one stuck its head through a hole in the net. Then they counted, "One, two, three," and flapped their wings in unison. The net rose up and they flew to a nearby thorn bush. The net stuck on the thorns and each quail dropped through its hole and escaped. The hunter was left to pick the thorns from his empty net.

For about a week the quail used the same trick to escape from the net. Day after day, the hunter went home empty-handed. His family grew worried. "What will become of us?" they asked. "You may never catch a bird again."

"Those quail have begun to cooperate and work together," he replied. "But they may not always live in such harmony. Then I will bag a lot of them again."

The next day, while landing at the feeding ground, one quail accidentally stepped on the head of another quail. "Why did you step on my head?" shouted the first quail.

"Oh, be quiet," said the second. "It was just a mistake. There's no need to shout at me."

"Well, why don't you watch where you're going?" shouted the first.

"Maybe you should watch where you're going so you won't get in my way again!" shouted the second.

Soon a noisy quarrel began with some quail taking the side of the first one and some taking the side of the second quail. At this point the first quail added, "And it's not fair that I have to carry the whole weight of the net while you lazy birds just watch me."

"Oh, ho!" shouted the second bird. "So you think you carry the net by yourself? Have you ever seen how much of the net I carry? It's a lot more than your part." And so the quail argued back and forth but to no avail.

A few days later, the hunter returned to the forest. He whistled and the quail flocked to him as usual. As soon as the net was over them, the second quail said to the first, "OK, strong boy. Let's see you lift the net by yourself."

"Not I," said the first quail. "I heard you say that you were the strongest. Go ahead and lift it yourself."

The other quail all joined in the argument as they had before. While they were arguing, the hunter gathered the four corners of the net and took the quail home with him. They were still arguing.

When we act from selfish greed,
We soon forget our common need.
We find ourselves in danger, all.
United we stand, divided we fall!

March

In March the wind blows loud and strong,
It roars among the trees.
It sings a wild exultant song,
Like waves on stormy seas.
The tossing branches madly strive,
The treetops bow before its drive.
Assaulted by the frantic gale,
The slender branches yield.
It seems their strength cannot prevail
On such a battlefield.
Yet when the wind is spent and gone,
Unharmed, the frail young buds live on.

- Molly de Havas

Rain

The rain is falling all around,
It falls on field and tree,
It rains on the umbrellas here,
And on the ships at sea.

- R. L. Stevenson

Chickadee

Elisabeth Lebret

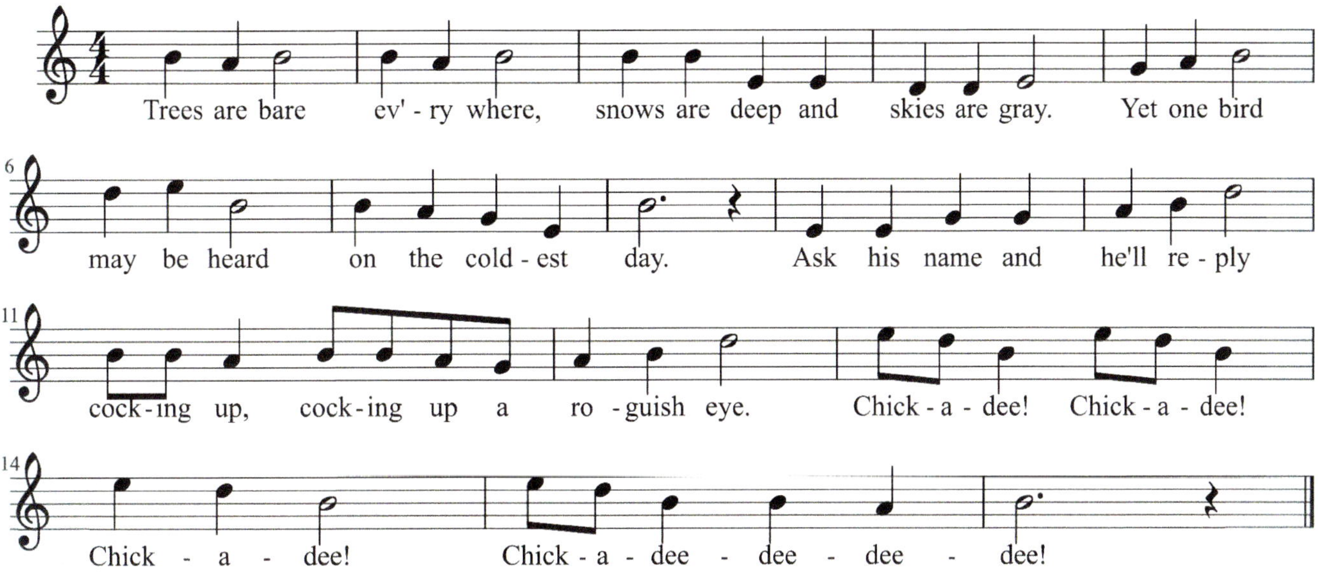

Spring

March Wind

Maud Usehold from "Year Round"

Elisabeth Lebret

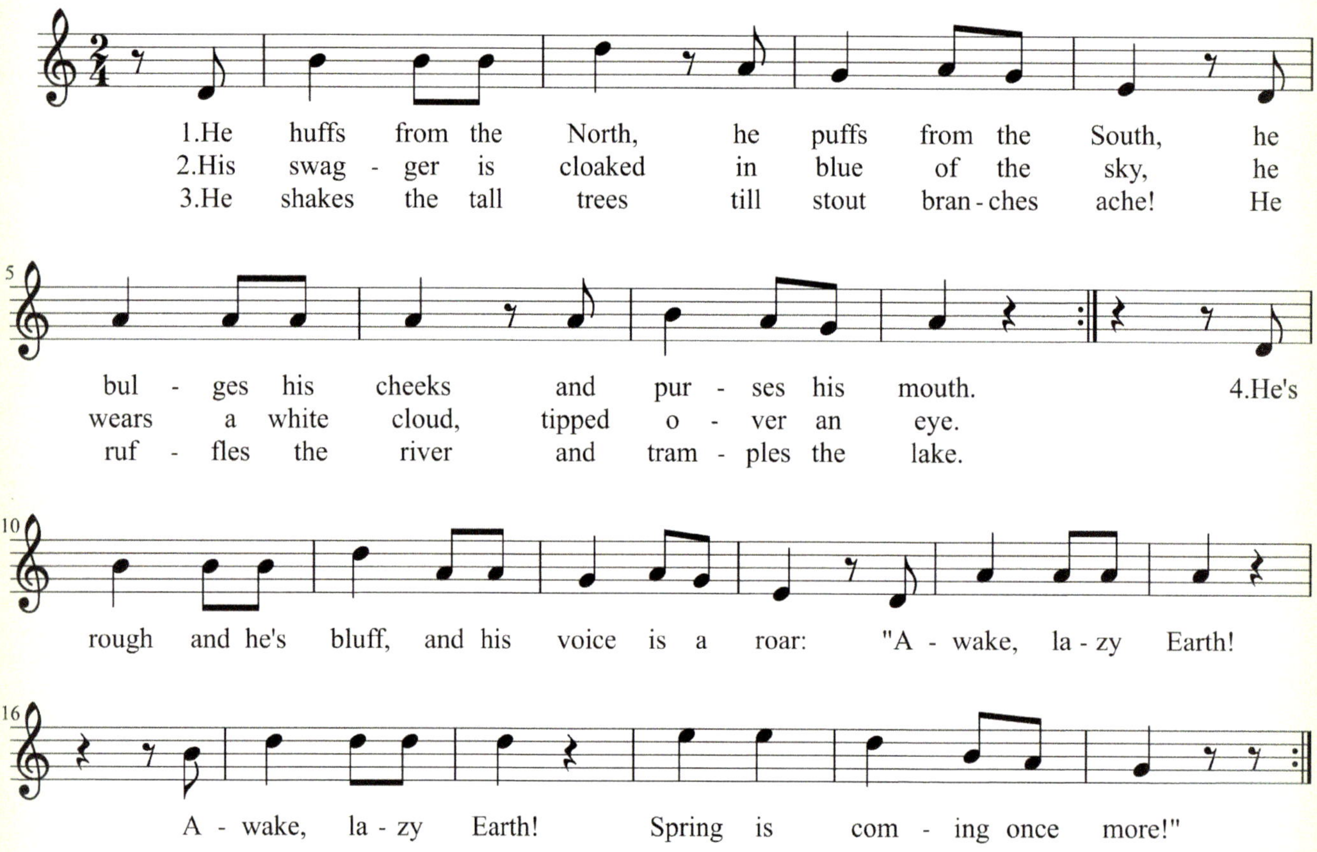

Spring Is Coming!

Elisabeth Lebret

The Waddlers

Said the Drake to his Lady one very wet day,
While he and she waddled and splashed on their way:
"You really should know how absurd you appear!
If you could just see yourself from the rear!
You rock and you roll from left side to right,
You slap your feet down – Oh, you are a sight!"
The Drake walked ahead and the Duck fell behind,
And watching him closely, she said: "He is blind!
The way that he waddles, he charges to me!
My dignified walk he simply can't see.
But, rocking and rolling, in side to side sway,
He actually dreams that *I* walk that way!"
She paused for a moment to shake her tail dry,
Then paddled along with a very deep sigh.
"No chance to correct him," she said: "I won't try!"

- Olin Wannamaker

About the Little Violet and the Big Blue Sky

by Rudolf Steiner

Once upon a time in a wood, where the sun made its way down through the trees, there grew a Little Violet, a modest Violet, under a tree that had big leaves. And the Violet could look up through the opening made by the tree-tops. As the Little Violet looked up through the wide opening in the woods, she saw the Big Blue Sky. The Little Violet saw the Blue Sky for the first time, for she had only just bloomed on the morning of that very day. Now the Violet trembled when she saw the Blue Sky and felt great fear. But she did not yet know why she felt such great fear.

Just then a Dog ran by – not a good Dog, but a savage wicked-looking one. And the Little Violet asked the Dog, "Tell me now, what is that overhead – that blue thing that is so like me?" For there was the Blue Sky, blue, just like the Little Violet.

And the Dog in his wickedness said, "Oh, that is a giant violet, and that violet has grown so large in order that it may crush you with all its might."

Then the Little Violet was still more frightened, thinking that the giant violet overhead had grown so large in order to strike her. And she drew her flower-leaves close together and no longer wished to look up at the giant violet. And she hid herself under a large leaf which had just been blown down by a gust of wind. So she stayed the whole day, hiding in terror from the Big Blue Sky.

In the morning the Little Violet crept out from under the leaf. Now, violets grow tired when they sleep and do not grow tired when they do not sleep. So the Little Violet was not at all tired, for she had been wondering the whole night through and was fresh and not weary. The first thing she saw was the rising sun and the red dawn. And when the Little Violet saw the red dawn, she was not at all afraid. She was glad inside and happy because of the red dawn.

Little by little the red dawn faded, and the pale blue sky came out once more. It grew bluer and bluer and the Little Violet thought again of what the Dog had said – that it was a giant violet which would crush her.

But all at once, a Lamb came by, and now the Little Violet wanted to ask again what that was overhead. "What is that up there?" asked the Little Violet.

And the Lamb said, "That is a great violet, blue, just like you."

Now the Little Violet was frightened again, thinking that she would have the same answer from the Lamb as from the wicked Dog. But the Lamb was gentle and good, and because it looked at her with such good and gentle eyes, the Little Violet asked one more question, "Oh, my dear Lamb, will the great violet up there crush me?"

"Oh, no," answered the Lamb. "It will not crush you! It is a great violet, and its love is much greater than your own love, as its own blueness is greater than the blue of your tiny form."

The Little Violet understood at once that the Big Blue Sky would never crush her, but instead had so much more blue in order to have so much more love. And the Little Violet understood that the Big Blue Sky would shield her from all that would do her harm in the world.

And then she felt so happy – the Little Violet – because all that she saw as blueness in the Big Blue Sky seemed to her like the love of God streaming towards her from every side. And the Little Violet always looked up, as if to pray to the God of the Violets.

- Translated by Virginia Field Birdsall
from The Waldorf School Reader

Now I Walk in Beauty

Native American Traditional

I Wander'd Lonely as a Cloud

I wander'd lonely as a cloud
That floats on high o'er vales and hills,
When all at once I saw a crowd,
A host of golden daffodils;
Beside the lake, beneath the trees,
Fluttering and dancing in the breeze.

Continuous as the stars that shine
And twinkle on the Milky Way,
They stretch'd in never-ending line
Along the margin of a bay:
Ten thousand saw I at a glance,
Tossing their heads in sprightly dance.

The waves beside them danced; but they
Out-did the sparkling waves in glee:
A poet could not but be gay,
In such a jocund company:
I gazed – and gazed – but little thought
What wealth the show to me had brought:

For oft, when on my couch I lie
In vacant or in pensive mood,
They flash upon that inward eye
Which is the bliss of solitude;
And then my heart with pleasure fills,
And dances with the daffodils.

- William Wordsworth

A Lion, a Hyena, and a Wolf

A legend from Africa

Once upon a time a lion, a hyena, and a wolf went out walking together. They met an antelope, and one of the three animals killed it. Now the food was to be divided among the three. The lion said to the hyena, "You divide it up!"

The hyena, afraid, and usually more concerned with the dead, answered, "We will divide the antelope into three equal shares. You will get one share, lion, one share for the wolf, and I, the hyena, will get one share."

When the lion heard this suggestion, he attacked the hyena and ate him up. Then the lion said to the frightened wolf, "Look, my dear wolf, we must divide differently now. How would you divide it?"

The wolf said, "Yes, we must divide it differently, as each one cannot receive the same as before. Since you have freed us from the hyena, you will get the first third. You would have received the second third in any case, and you must also receive the third, as you are the wisest and bravest animal of all!" This was how the wolf divided it up.

The lion asked him, "Who taught you to divide like that?"

The wolf said, "The hyena taught me to divide like that!" The lion took the three shares and did not eat the wolf.

The Tortoise and the Hare

Alan Howard

Elisabeth Lebret

sleep on some hay, was dream - ing how fast he'd get there.
Tor - toise said noth - ing, still kept on his way, nor wast - ed a thought on the
hare, who, when he ar-rived at the end of the day, found the tor - toise...
found the tor - toise... was al - read - y, was al - read - y... was al-read - y...
There!

Duck's Ditty

All along the backwater,
Through the rushes tall,
Ducks are a-dabbling,
Up tails, all!

Ducks' tails, drakes' tails,
Yellow feet a-quiver,
Yellow bills all out of sight,
Busy in the river!

Slushy green undergrowth
Where the roach swim –
Here we keep our larder
Cool and full and dim.

Everyone for what he likes!
We like to be
Heads down, tails up,
Dabbling free!

High in the blue above
Swifts whirl and call –
We are down a-dabbling,
Up tails, all!

- *Kenneth Grahame*

Summer

The Bunch of Flowers

By Rudolf Steiner

Once there were two children who took a walk one Sunday. On the way home each one of them carried a bunch of flowers. One child said, "Oh, but my flowers are beautiful!"

The other said, "And mine are beautiful, too!" Each one liked only his own bunch of flowers. But the bunch of the one child did not please the other child at all. The one child had in his bunch some beautiful flowers, full of sweet perfume, but also the common grass, sheaves of field grain, and even thistles.

The other child had only sweet-smelling flowers, nothing but sweet flowers, and so this child with the sweet flowers said to the other, "Do you know, your bunch of flowers has every possible kind of blossom in it? I do not like it at all!" And the other child did not like the bunch that had only sweet-smelling flowers in it.

How do you think, dear children, that the story continues? The child with the bunch containing sheaves of grain and thistles told the other child a story. Listen to what he said:

"One other time I was out walking on a Sunday, and out there in the open, I fell asleep and dreamed. But what did I dream? Listen. I lay in the meadow" – so the child said – "and there came great animals and small animals, and they talked to each other. There was an altogether strange, very, very small, quite tiny animal and a large animal. The tiny, little animal was a Bee, the large one was a Calf, and

Calf and Bee talked together. The Bee said, 'O you Calf, you understand nothing at all about the plants, but I, I understand everything. I know which plants are sweet, and from these I sip honey. The honey I take then to people, and people love the honey so much! If I should not fly to all the beautiful flowers with their lovely scent, there would be no honey for them.'

"Then spoke the Calf: 'Do you know, I could not live only from the sweet-scented flowers which taste so good to you. All the flowers over which you fly quite carelessly – these I must eat. And if I should not eat them, there would be no milk in the world. And without milk, people could not be nourished, and then no honey would be needed, for there would be no one to enjoy it!' "

In this fashion the two children conversed. And the child who had the bunch of sweet flowers understood that there was something for him to learn. The other child had already learned what was right through his dream. What the child with the sweet flowers realized is that there cannot be only sweet flowers. He understood that there must be all sorts of different flowers, all working together.

And so the child learned to love the bunch which held every possible kind of plant. And the child who had gone to sleep and dreamed could say, "Yes, that is what the Calf said. There are certain kinds of flowers and then there are other kinds of flowers, but all of them are necessary, and therefore a bouquet with all kinds of flowers is much more worthwhile and precious than one which has only sweet flowers."

Now, my dear children, when you go to school, it is as if you went walking on a beautiful Sunday, and from school you can take with you all the most precious things out into life. And when you can take with you into life a bouquet of flowers from all that your dear teachers have taught you, you will have the greatest joy in such a bouquet. But it must contain all the flowers, not only the sweet-smelling ones! This you must learn: that you take into yourselves sometimes something that is not exactly sweet! If you study earnestly and industriously, you will notice that into your later life you will have not only a bunch of sweet flowers, but a bunch of those life-filled flowers upon which your life depends.

Think this over, my dear children, so that each time your teachers ask something difficult of you, you obey them lovingly. From school you will receive the most beautiful bouquet of flowers for your whole life, and it will give you the most pleasure if it contains all the different plants of life. Each memory of your school years will give you strength for life itself. For human beings, when they are grown up, win the finest forces for their lives when they can take with them from their school such a bunch of flowers. They are life forces which endure until death — and even beyond death.

- Translated by Virginia Field Birdsall

The Browny Hen

A browny hen sat on her nest,
With a hey-ho for the springtime!
Seven brown eggs 'neath her downy breast,
With a hey-ho for the springtime!
A brown hen clucks all day from dawn,
With a hey-ho for the springtime!
She's seven wee chicks as yellow as corn,
With a hey-ho for the springtime!

- Irene F. Fawsey

The Eagle

He clasps the crag with crooked hands;
Close to the sun in lonely lands,
Ring'd with the azure world, he stands.

The wrinkled sea beneath him crawls;
He watches from his mountain walls,
And like a thunderbolt he falls.

– Alfred, Lord Tennyson

Praise

Molly de Havas *Anonymous*

The Rune of St. Patrick

At Tara today in this fateful hour
I place all heaven with its power,
And the sun with its brightness,
And the snow with its whiteness,
And fire with all the strength it hath,
And lightning with its rapid wrath,
And the winds with their swiftness along their path,
And the sea with its deepness,
And the rocks with their steepness,
And the earth with its starkness:
All these I place,
By God's almighty help and grace,
Between myself and the powers of darkness.

The Dwarfs

Molly de Havas *Elisabeth Lebret*

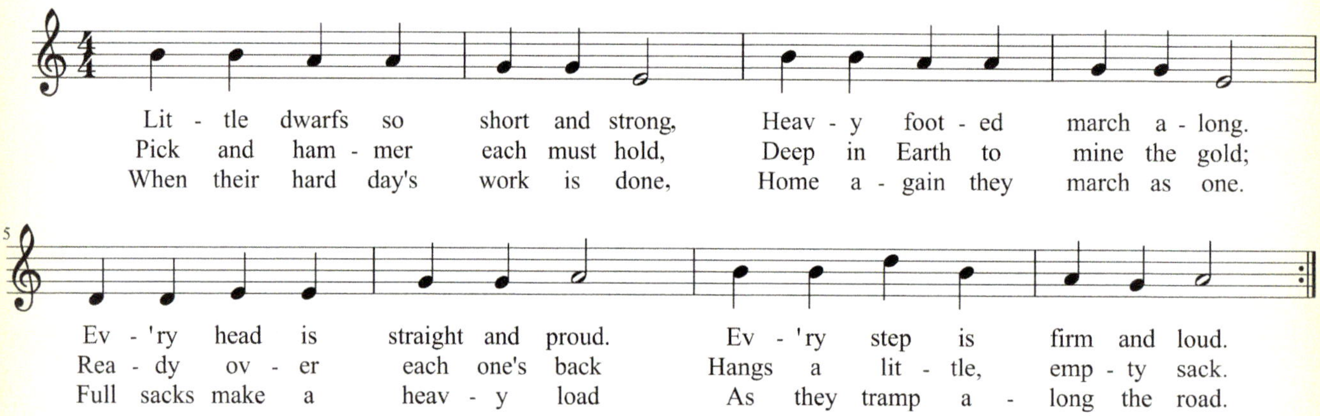

Nicholas Nye

Thistle and darnel and dock grew there,
    And a bush, in the corner, of may,
On the orchard wall I used to sprawl
    In the blazing heat of the day;
Half asleep and half awake,
    While the birds went twittering by,
And nobody there my lone to share
    But Nicholas Nye.

Nicholas Nye was lean and gray,
    Lame of leg and old,
More than a score of donkey's years
    He had seen since he was foaled;
He munched the thistles, purple and spiked,
    Would sometimes stoop and sigh,
And turn his head, as if he said,
    'Poor Nicholas Nye!'

Alone with his shadow he'd drowse in the meadow,
    Lazily swinging his tail,
At break of day he used to bray, –
    Not much too hearty and hale;

But a wonderful gumption was under his skin,
    And a clear calm light in his eye,
And once in a while: he'd smile ...
    Would Nicholas Nye.

Seem to be smiling at me, he would,
    From his bush in the corner, of may, –
Bony and ownerless, widowed and worn,
    Knobble-kneed, lonely and grey;
And over the grass would seem to pass
    'Neath the deep dark blue of the sky,
Something much better than words between me
    And Nicholas Nye.

But dusk would come in the apple boughs,
    The green of the glow-worm shine,
The birds in nest would crouch to rest,
    And home I'd trudge to mine;
And there, in the moonlight, dark with dew,
    Asking not wherefore nor why,
Would brood like a ghost, and as still as a post,
    Old Nicholas Nye.

- *Walter de la Mare*

Summer Is Ending

"Summer is ending," the father bear said.
"In yonder tree hollow I'll make me a bed."

"Summer is ending," said all the gold weeds.
And so, softly sighing, they scattered their seeds.

"Summer is ending," the hurricane cried,
Hurling and whirling harsh rains high and wide.

"Summer is ending," said Old Father Sun.
"My flame must grow fainter, then fade out to none."

Beauty and the Beast

Once upon a time a rich Merchant, meeting with heavy losses, had to retire to a small cottage with his three daughters. The two elder grumbled at this, but the youngest, named Beauty, tried to comfort her father. Once when he was going on a journey to try to mend his fortunes, the two elder girls told him to bring them some handsome presents, but Beauty begged him to bring her only a rose.

When the Merchant was on his way home, he saw some fine roses and, thinking of Beauty, plucked the prettiest he could find. He had no sooner taken it than he saw a hideous Beast, who asked him how he dared to touch his flowers and talked of putting him to death. The Merchant pleaded that he had only plucked the rose for his daughter, Beauty.

"Well," said the Beast gruffly, "I will not take your life if you will bring one of your daughters here to die in your stead. She must come willingly, or I will not have her."

The Merchant returned home in great sorrow. When he came near his house, his daughters came out to greet him, but seeing the sadness of his face, they asked the cause of his trouble. Giving Beauty the rose, he told her all. The two elder sisters laid all the blame on Beauty and said that she alone must suffer, as she was the cause of this misfortune. In spite of the entreaties of her father, Beauty set out with him for the Beast's palace, to the secret joy of her two envious sisters.

When they arrived at the Beast's castle, the doors opened of themselves and sweet music was heard. Beauty and her father walked into a room where supper had been prepared. Just as they finished their meal, the Beast entered and said in a mild tone, "Beauty, did you come here willingly?"

"Yes, willingly," she answered in a trembling voice.

"So much the better for you," said the Beast. "Your father must return home in the morning."

Beauty tried to cheer her father at parting, but he left her with a heavy heart. After he had gone, she began to explore the palace. She found a fine room, on the door of which was written in gold letters "Beauty's Room." All her meals were served to the sound of music, and at suppertime the Beast appeared and talked so pleasantly that she soon lost her fear of him.

One day, the Beast turned to Beauty and asked, "Am I so very ugly?"

"Yes, indeed you are," said Beauty. "But you are so kind that I do not mind your looks."

"Will you marry me, then?" the Beast asked.

Beauty, looking away, said, "Pray do not ask me." With a sad voice, the Beast then bade her good night and retired.

The palace was full of beautiful rooms and Beauty had everything she could wish for, but except at suppertime, she was always alone. The Beast then appeared and behaved so agreeably that she grew to like him more and more. But when he asked, "Beauty, will you marry me?" she always replied, "No," at which he sadly took his leave.

Although Beauty had all she wanted, she was not happy, as she missed her father and sisters. At last, one evening, she begged so hard of the Beast to let her go home that he agreed on her promise not to stay away longer than two months. He gave her a ring and told her to place it on her dressing table whenever she wished to go or to return, and he also gave her presents to take home with her.

The poor Beast looked sadder than ever when he said farewell to Beauty. She tried to cheer him, but nothing she said could comfort him. That night Beauty put the ring on her dressing table and fell asleep.

The next morning when she awoke, what was her joy at finding herself in her father's house with the gifts from the palace at her bedside! Her father was overjoyed to see her again, and her two sisters pretended to be glad, but they were secretly jealous of her good fortune. Time passed very pleasantly. Whenever Beauty said she must return, her father begged her to stay a few days longer, and she could not resist his entreaties.

But one night, she dreamed that the poor Beast was lying dead in the palace garden. She awoke in a fright, looked for her ring and placed in on her dressing table. In the morning she was at the palace again, but the Beast was nowhere to be found. Finally she ran to the place in the garden in her dream, and there, sure enough, was the poor Beast, lying on his back, senseless.

At this sight Beauty wept and reproached herself for having caused his death. She ran to the fountain and sprinkled his face with water. The Beast opened his eyes and as soon as he could speak, he said sorrowfully, "Now that I see you once more, I die contented."

"No, no," she cried. "You shall not die! I will marry you!"

The moment Beauty uttered these words, a dazzling light shone everywhere, the palace windows glittered with lamps, and music was heard around. To her great wonder, a handsome young Prince stood before her, who said that her words had broken the spell of a magician, by which he had been doomed to take the form of a Beast until a beautiful girl should love him in spite of his ugliness.

The grateful Prince now claimed Beauty for his wife. The Merchant was soon informed of his daughter's good fortune, and the Prince and Beauty were married on the following day.

The Crystal Ball

Once upon a time...

There was once an enchantress, who had three sons who loved each other as brothers. But the old woman did not trust them and thought they wanted to steal her power from her. So she changed the eldest into an eagle, which was forced to dwell in the rocky mountains, and was often seen flying in great circles in the sky. The second, she changed into a whale, which lived in the deep sea, and all that was seen of it was that it sometimes spouted up a great jet of water in the air. Each of them bore his human form for only two hours a day.

The third son, who was afraid she might change him into a raging wild beast—a bear perhaps, or a wolf—went secretly away. He had heard that a king's daughter, who was bewitched and imprisoned in the castle of the golden sun, was waiting to be set free. Those who tried to free her, however, risked their lives. Three-and-twenty youths had already died a miserable death, and now only one other might make the attempt, after which no more must come. And as the third son's heart was without fear, he made up his mind to seek out the castle of the golden sun.

He had already traveled about for a long time without being able to find it, when he came by chance into a great forest and could not find the way out of it. All at once he saw in the distance two giants, who made a sign to him with their hands. When he came up to them, they said, "We are quarreling about a cap, and which of us it is to belong to. And as we are equally strong, neither of us can get the better of the other. Small men are cleverer than we are, so we will leave the decision to you."

"How can you dispute about an old cap?" said the youth.

"You do not know what properties it has. It is a wishing-cap. Whosoever puts it on can wish himself away to wherever he wishes to go, and in an instant he will be there," said one of the giants.

"Give me the cap," said the youth. "I will go a short distance off, and when I call you, you must run a race. The cap shall belong to the one who gets to me first." Then the youth put on the cap and walked away. He thought of the king's daughter, forgot the giants, and walked onward.

At length he sighed from the very bottom of his heart and cried, "Ah, if I were but at the castle of the golden sun." Hardly had the words passed his lips than he was standing on a high mountain before the gate of the castle.

He entered and went through all the rooms, until in the last he found the king's daughter. How shocked he was when he saw her. She had bleary eyes, red hair, and an ashen-gray face full of wrinkles. "Are you the king's daughter, whose beauty the whole world praises?" cried he.

"Ah," she answered, "this is not my true form. Human eyes can see me only in this state of ugliness. But that you may know what I am like, look in the mirror—it cannot be misled, and it will show you my image as it is in truth." She gave him the mirror in his hand, and he saw therein the likeness of the most beautiful maiden on earth. He saw, too, how the tears were rolling down her cheeks with grief.

Then said he, "How can you be set free? I fear no danger."

She replied, "He who gets the crystal ball and holds it before the enchanter will destroy his power with it, and I shall resume my true form. But," she added, "so many have already failed and gone to meet death for this. You are so young, I grieve that you should encounter such great danger."

"Nothing can keep me from doing it," said he. "But tell me what I must do."

"You shall know everything," said the king's daughter. "When you descend the mountain on which the castle stands, a wild bull will stand below by a spring, and you must fight with it. If you have the luck to kill it, a fiery bird will spring out of it, which bears in its body a red-hot egg. In the egg, the crystal ball lies as its yolk. The bird, however, will not let the egg fall until forced to do so, and if the egg falls on the ground, it will flame up and burn everything that is near. Even the egg itself will melt, and with it the crystal ball. Then your trouble will have been in vain."

The youth went down to the spring, where the bull snorted and bellowed at him. After a long struggle the youth plunged his sword into the animal's body, and it fell down. Instantly a fiery bird arose from it and was about to fly away, but the first brother, the eagle, was passing between the clouds. He swooped down, hunted the bird away to the sea, and struck it with his beak until, in its pain, it let the egg fall.

The egg, however, did not fall into the sea, but onto a fisherman's hut which stood on the shore. The hut began at once to smoke and was about to break into flames. Then arose in the sea waves as high as a house, which streamed over the hut and subdued the fire. The second brother, the whale, had come swimming to them and had driven the water up on high.

When the fire was extinguished, the youth sought for the egg and happily found it. It was not yet melted, but the shell had broken from being so suddenly cooled with the sea water, and he could take out the crystal ball unharmed.

When the youth went before the enchanter and held the crystal ball before him, the enchanter said, "My power is destroyed, and from this time forth, you are the king of the castle of the golden sun. With this you can likewise give back to your brothers their human forms."

Then the youth hastened to the king's daughter, and when he entered the room, she was standing there in the full splendor of her beauty. Joyfully they exchanged rings with each other.

In Closing

Giving Thanks

The sun has kissed the apples red
And turned the pumpkins yellow.
The gobbling turkeys are well fed
And purple grapes are mellow.
The squirrels' nests are full of nuts,
The farmers' barns spill over
With ripened corn and wheat and oats
From fields the snow will cover.
The little birds find each dried pod
Holds food in coldest weather;
So man and beast give thanks to God,
Who feeds them all together.

– Margaret Peckham

Silver

Slowly, silently, now the moon
Walks the night in her silver shoon;
This way and that, she peers and sees
Silver fruit upon silver trees;
One by one the casements catch
Her beams beneath the silvery thatch;
Couched in his kennel, like a log
With paws of silver sleeps the dog;
From their shadowy cote the white breasts peep
Of doves in a silver-feathered sleep;
A harvest mouse goes scampering by,

With silver claws and a silver eye;
And moveless fish in the water gleam,
By silver reeds in a silver stream.

- Walter de la Mare

Main Lesson Is Ended

There lives in me an image
Of all that I should be;
Until I have become it
My heart is never free.

I Strive to Learn

I strive to learn,
To learn to give,
To give my heart
To all I see.
I see that I,
With heart aflame,
Aflame with love,
Can light the world.

– Rudolf Copple

At the Ringing of the Bells

To wonder at beauty,
Stand guard over truth,
Look up to the noble,
Decide for the good,
Leads man on his journey
For goals in his life:
To strength in his willing,
To peace in his feeling,
To light in his thought;
And teaches him trust
In the guidance of God,
In all that there is
In the world-wide all,
In the soul's deep soil.

– *Rudolf Steiner*

At the Ringing of the Bells

Rudolf Steiner — Merwin Lewis

Vo.
Pno.
And teach-es us trust in the work-ing of God, in all that there
is, in the widths of the world, in the depths
of the soul, in the depths of the
soul.

Evening Prayer

From my head to my feet
I am the image of God;
From my heart to my hands
I feel the breath of God;
When I speak with my mouth,
I follow God's will.
When I behold God everywhere –
In mother, in father,
In all dear people,
In flower and animal,
In tree and stone –
Nothing brings fear,
Just love
To all that is around me.

– Rudolf Steiner

Acknowledgments

To the children, parents and teachers reading this book:

Almost a hundred years ago, in the very first Waldorf school in Stuttgart, Germany, a teacher named Caroline von Heydebrand made a book of songs, poems and stories to help the children learn how to read. She called the book *Der Sonne Licht.* In Germany and Switzerland children still read that book. *The Sun with Loving Light* is like that first book. Imagine all the children, in countries all around the world where there are Waldorf schools today, reading books like that first reader!

Teachers in the first Waldorf school in the United States, the Rudolf Steiner School in New York City, made a reader too, designed like Caroline von Heydebrand's book. They called it *The Key to the Kingdom.* That book helped us in deciding about this book.

There are many people who work together to make a book like this, full of many poems, pictures, stories and songs. We thank all those who helped in gathering all the things needed for this reader.

Waldorf teachers, just like the teachers in your school now, have been writing verses, singing songs, and telling stories for many years. This made finding the best verses for this book possible, and we thank all of them. Some wrote the verses and have their names with their work, but many were written and used again and again by teachers and poets who gave their work to others without their names going with them. We thank all of those whose names we know and those we do not know for their fine work.

We thank the Waldorf School Association of Ontario in Canada for saving the songs of Elisabeth Lebret and for giving us permission to have many of her songs in this collection. We thank Molly de

Havas, Margaret Peckham, Eleanor Farjeon, Dorothy Harrer, Margret Meyerkort, Kenneth Grahame and all the poets, some still living, who have written many poems and who have their poems in this book.

We thank the editor, Stephen Bloomquist, a Waldorf teacher who has taught four classes at the Waldorf School of Lexington, and who knows what the right things are for children to read.

Special thanks go to Pamela Dalton, the artist who did the shadow pictures. Pamela has illustrated a number of books. Her work is always delicate and exciting to see. She delights in the beauty of the earth, animals, plants, and people, and she shows this in her pictures.

For the watercolor paintings of sunrise and sunset which appear at the beginning and end, we thank J. Ch. Mellinger Verlag GmbH, Stuttgart, Germany, for letting us use these pictures. These paintings are also in the German reader. So all young readers are looking at the same pictures!

Hansjörg Hofrichter is one who read *Der Sonne Licht* as a boy in a Waldorf school in Germany. When he found the book as a man, he made sure the book was published again so that children could read it once more. He thought a reader in English for America like this reader would be a wonderful thing, and he worked hard to help finish the project. The Waldorf Stiftung and the Rudolf und Clara Kreutzer Stiftung helped in bringing the book to children in America. Thanks are due to them, too.

Most importantly, we thank Rudolf Steiner, who told many of the stories and wrote some of the poems in this book. Rudolf Steiner gave us Waldorf education so that boys and girls everywhere could learn in a new way. This way makes the hard work of learning full of light and love so that children want to learn for their whole lives and not only in school.